To:

From:

Published by Hallmark Gift Books,
a division of Hallmark Cards, Inc.,
Kansas City, MO 64141
Visit us on the Web at www.Hallmark.com.

Editor: Chelsea Fogleman
Art Director: Kevin Swanson
Designer and Production Artist: Bryan Ring

ISBN: 978-1-59530-420-9
BOK1182

Printed and bound in China
JUL11

ShaRa Tiara
and the Frog Prints

Written by **Katherine Stano** • Illustrated by **Stacey Lamb**

Hallmark
GIFT BOOKS

Shara Tiara was
no ordinary princess.

Of course, she loved a fabulous ball, but her favorite kind wasn't a hoity-toity party most princesses adored. Shara was all about baseball.

She also had her own way of looking royal, despite what her classmates, Princess Cutesy and Princess Frou Frou, thought.

And to make matters extra unprincess-y,
Shara enjoyed playing with her frog friend, Sir Hop,
much more than any ol' prince!

One afternoon, as Shara and Sir Hop were playing catch, a great big raindrop plopped on Shara's head. THUD! SPLAT!

"Is it raining?" she asked. And before Sir Hop could answer, the sky rumbled and grumbled. A rainstorm crashed down.

Shara and Sir Hop ran toward the castle.

Once they were inside, Shara and Sir Hop became royally blue.
They couldn't play baseball in the rain!

Shara's mother, the queen, was walking by and saw their glum faces. "Why don't you try a new game?" she suggested. "It's just like I always say, one must remember to try new things! I bet if you put your heads together, you'll think of something."

After much pondering, Shara had a grand idea. "Want to play hide-and-seek?" she asked Sir Hop.

Sir Hop bounced up and down. "Sure!" But a moment later, the little frog looked confused. "What do you hide? What do you seek?"

Shara forgot that not all frogs knew how to play hide-and-seek. "I'll count to ten while you sneak away and hide. Then I'll search for you!" she said.

"I like this game already," said Sir Hop. Then he leapfrogged away!

As he hop, hop, hopped off, Sir Hop soon heard footsteps. It was Shara! Quickly, he got out of sight.

"Hmmm." She had a hunch about how to find Sir Hop. So she skipped down the hallway . . .

Shara zipped into the ballroom. (She always thought "ballroom" was a funny name for a room that you couldn't play baseball in.) "Aha!" she announced. But Sir Hop had vanished.

"Wow! Sir Hop sure has picked up on hide-and-seek quickly," said Shara.

Then, with a dainty ding-ding-ding, the snack bell rang. All this looking for Sir Hop had made Shara very hungry! She strolled off to the kitchen.

"Hello, Chef Sauté!"

"What shall I batter up for you, Your Little Highness?" he asked.

And because she was no ordinary princess, Shara replied, "Oh, I'll just make myself a peanut butter and jelly sandwich!"

Then she had a super bright idea.

Shara tiptoed into the dining room carrying a feast of goodies. She knew that Sir Hop couldn't resist snack time!

Soon the little frog sniffed something delicious. He raced to the table, where he found a beautiful sight—all kinds of yummy treats! He immediately began munching.

"Gotcha!" Shara said. She had finally caught up with the frog prince and his frog prints! Sir Hop jumped with surprise and landed in the ice cream. This caused the friends to giggle . . . and then giggle some more!

"You know what's really good with ice cream?" Shara asked. "French fries!"

"So are French FLIES," added Sir Hop.

Shara wasn't so sure about French flies, but she remembered what her mother had said: "One must remember to try new things."

Soon the sun came out, and Sir Hop asked Shara, "Think we can swing another game?"

"Yeah, let's go!" said Shara, grabbing her baseball and mitt.

Once outside, she threw the ball, but—oh, no!—it was about to hit a window!

"Whew!" said Shara.
"Sweet catch!"

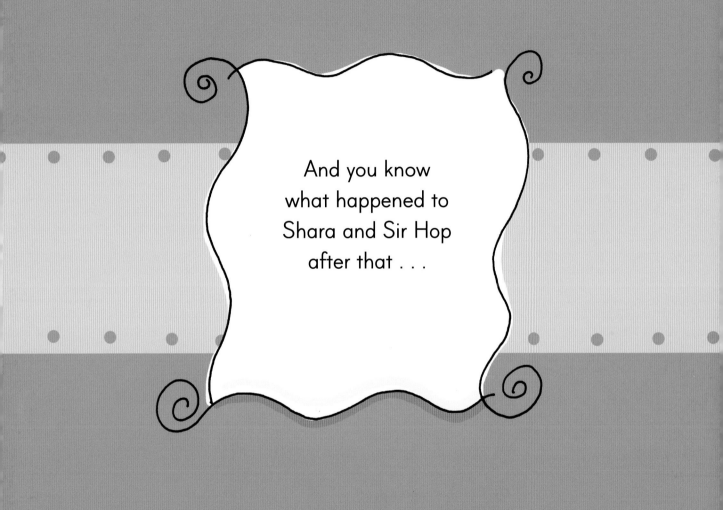

And you know
what happened to
Shara and Sir Hop
after that . . .

They had an absolute ball!

The End.

Did you like
this frog-and-princess
friendship story?

Please send your comments to:
Hallmark Book Feedback
P.O. Box 419034
Mail Drop 215
Kansas City, MO 64141

Or e-mail us at:
booknotes@hallmark.com